Jack

The Donkey Who Could See with His Ears

ISBN: 978-1-957809-54-0

Published by Cornerstone Creativity Groups LLC
info@thecornerstonepublishers.com

Dedication

To Kevin Brown.

Photos courtesy of US Blind Hockey Team

Jack wasn't your regular donkey. He had goals and the major one was becoming a hockey player. However, there was one problem. Jack was born with a rare disease that affected his eyesight and by the time he was 5 years old he lost his sight permanently. Jack didn't let that define him. He loved to play sports and his eyes didn't stop him from playing every single sport his brother, Brent, could play. In fact he was as good as his brother, but Jack's real dream was to play hockey.

One cold morning, Jack's father, Henry, walked into the kitchen and looked out the window to see his youngest son, Jack sitting on the bench with all his hockey gear on listening to his brother, Brent and the other boys as they played hockey. They wouldn't let Jack play because he could not see. Jack wore thick black rimmed glasses to protect his eyes from things getting in his eye, like dust and dirt. Henry's heart broke for Jack. All Jack ever talked about was hockey.

Henry could hear what the other boys said about Jack. They called him names like 4-eyes, clumsy weird-o. Henry was determined to figure out a way to get Jack on the ice playing the game he loved the most and protect his glasses. Henry was an Engineer so he knew he could figure something out. He went to his workroom and began to figure out a plan.

After about 2 weeks Henry had a plan and he could not wait to share it with Jack. Henry walked into Jacks room, “Good Morning Jack. I have a surprise for you” he said. Jack sat up with excitement. “We are going to be learning how to play hockey” His father announced and Jack jumped out of bed. “Really Dad? You will do that for me?” Jack asked with a smile on his face. “What about my glasses?” “Don’t worry Jack I have it all figured out. I have created a special helmet to protect your glasses!”

The following day Jack's father rented out the local hockey rink so just the two of them could get to work. Jack was excited but he was also worried. "Dad, how will I know where the puck is?" He asked and his father laughed.

“I have created a special hockey puck for you,” His father said and brought out a hockey puck. It had four little bells around it and was bigger than the regular puck. Jack giggled as he shook the puck, and the bells rang together. “All you need to do is follow the sound!” His father encouraged and Jack nodded with a determined look on his face. Jack may not be able to see, but his hearing was enhanced so Jack could hear things a lot better and sharper than other people.

Soon, Jacks friends from the neighborhood came into the rink and Jack was surprised. “Why are they here?” He asked as he heard his friend’s voices and his father laughed. “You need a team, Jack. This is your team! You are playing with people who love you and believe in you.”

The team trained for six months, every day. They were exhausted after training, but their love for hockey and Jack kept them going. Jack had some difficulties at the beginning. He would trip and fall, he skated into the goal one time and he missed the puck a lot but, with time, he caught up and became a good player. Even though his team members had perfect eyesight, Jacks sense of hearing was heightened, and he was a super-fast skater, so those two qualities made Jack the teams “secret weapon.” “We have been invited for a tournament,” Jack’s father announced one evening while they trained, and everyone froze. Jack couldn’t speak. He was scared, scared about the possibilities of participating in a tournament where all other players could see.

“You don’t have to worry Jack. They are using our hockey puck. We have been training for this! Jack, trust your teammates and trust in yourself. They have got you covered and so do I! “Do you trust us?” Jack’s father asked. They had this dream to play hockey for months and have been practicing every day. The opportunity is now at their doorsteps. They couldn’t back down now. With his voice shaking, Jack said, “we’ll play, Dad. We’ll play our best!” The entire team burst out into cheers! “That’s the spirit!” Henry said and they trained intensively for the next few weeks.

The tournament came and their team's name was THE ACHIEVERS. They didn't look intimidating but once they got on the ice, they DOMINATED. Everyone saw that Jack had AMAZING talent even with his disability. He scored the winning goal of the tournament and was the most valuable player in the competition.

All Jack needed to succeed was to believe in himself, practice hard, have the love and support of his father and his friends for his dream to play hockey to come true.

NOTE

NOTE

www.ingramcontent.com/pod-product-compliance
Lightning Source LLC
LaVergne TN
LVHW070210110826
845147LV00002B/554
9781957809540